"The name's Ventura...Ace Ventura, pet detective. I'm here to take you home to your mommy. Do you want to see your mommy?"

"Arf, arf," the dog answered. He wagged his tail excitedly.

Ace Ventura turned the ignition key. The car's engine chugged once, but did not start. Ace sat back for a moment and looked out the windshield.

Standing outside the car was a very large man carrying a very large baseball bat. And he didn't look very happy!

"Ya little creep," the big man howled. "Gimme that dog!"

Smash!

The windshield broke as the bat landed.

"Oh, boy," Ace said.

"Arf!" barked the pooch.

Join Ace on all his missions
to serve and protect animals everywhere!

ACE VENTURA: PET DETECTIVE

ACE VENTURA: WHEN NATURE CALLS

Adapted by Marc Cerasini

Based on the screenplay by
Jack Bernstein and
Tom Shadyac & Jim Carrey
and the story by Jack Bernstein

Bullseye Books
Random House New York

1

Tools of the Trade

A man in a brown delivery uniform strolled down a Miami street. It was a warm Florida afternoon. The sky was bright blue. The beaches were filled with sunbathers.

The man wished he could join the fun. But he had something more important to do. *Much* more important.

The man's brown uniform bulged where his large potbelly hung over his belt. He wore a baseball hat with the letters HDS on it. He also had a big smile on his face for everyone he met. A big, toothy, *goofy* smile.

The man carried a box with lots of stickers on it. GLASS—CONTENTS FRAGILE! warned one sticker. HANDLE WITH CARE read another.

But the man didn't seem to pay much attention to these stickers. He spun the box on his fingertips. The box tumbled out of his hand, but he caught it before it hit the ground. Seconds later, he almost dropped it again. But again, he caught it just in time.

"Whew, that was close!" the delivery guy said. Then he spun around and slammed the box against a wall. A tinkling sound could be heard inside the package.

"Good *morning!*" he said, greeting the people he passed on the street. He gave everyone a wink or a nod.

"Hello!" he bellowed. "Handy Delivery Service! Really grrrreatt to see ya! And what a bea-U-ti-ful day!"

Most people looked at the man as if he were crazy. Others crossed the street to get out of his way. This didn't bother the deliveryman! He just continued on his merry way.

After a couple more steps, he spun the package again. Then he threw it up in the air. He put his hands out to catch it—and missed!

The box hit the pavement with a sickening crash. Everyone turned to look. They all could hear the sound of breaking glass.

"Oops!" said the deliveryman. Embarrassed, he bent down to pick up the box.

But when he tried to grab it, he missed again. He kicked it instead. The brown package flew through the air. It bounced off a palm tree in someone's yard. The sound of pulverized glass was even louder than before.

The deliveryman ran into the yard and picked up the package. It was dented and crushed. He shook it once, his ear to the box. When he heard the tinkle inside, he smiled and nodded his head. He ambled away, pleased with himself. The box rattled with each step the deliveryman took.

He rounded a corner to find a huge apartment building in front of him. He squinted. Then he looked at the address label, and back at the building.

"Well, righty-ho!" he said to no one in particular. "This is the place!"

A bunch of kids were playing street football in front of the building.

"Hey, kids!" the deliveryman shouted. "Go out for a long one!"

With that, he hurled the package like a football. All the kids stopped playing, but

3

none of them tried to catch the box.

It landed in the street with a *crunch!*

"Okay! Nice try! You kids have a dandy day! And play safely," the deliveryman said as he scooped up the dented box.

He blew some dust off the brown paper wrapping and went into the building.

As the deliveryman crossed the lobby, he gave everyone a big smile and a hello. Then he spotted the elevator. It was already crowded with people. He jumped inside, just as the automatic doors began to close. The HDS man made it...but the package didn't.

Crunch! The doors closed on the box. The elevator doors opened and closed again. And again the box was crushed between them.

"Oops!" said the deliveryman. He rolled his eyes and pulled the box into the elevator. The doors finally closed.

Ding! The elevator doors opened on the third floor. As soon as they did, the HDS man threw his package into the hallway. He bounded out of the elevator. This time he played soccer with the box. He kicked it down the hall. It bounced off the walls and rolled around with a loud shattering sound.

Suddenly the deliveryman stopped. He'd caught sight of a door at the end of the hall. The door had the number 311 on it.

"Okay!" he said. He pointed at the door and hollered, "We're going *downtown!*"

He kicked the box one last time. *Wham!*

The package flew through the air and landed hard in front of 311. The HDS man smiled his big goofy smile. He pulled his cap down tight. He pulled his collar up. Then he sauntered to the door.

Knock, knock, knock!

A little dog inside the apartment began to bark.

"Shut up, ya stupid mutt!" shouted a surly voice from behind the door. The deliveryman knocked again.

"Who is it...and whaddaya want?" yelled the man behind the door.

"Handy Delivery Service, sir. And how are you this fine afternoon? All rightee then."

The door flew open to reveal a tall, burly

man. He wore a dirty T-shirt and had a scruffy beard. He was very, very big. At the big man's feet was a little fluffy white dog. The dog had a pink nose and shiny black eyes.

"*Arf, arf,*" barked the dog. The delivery guy looked down at the dog. Then he looked back up at the tall man.

"Package for you, sir," he said with a smile, thrusting the crushed and dented box into the man's arms, which were covered with tattoos.

The big man took the package, then shook it. The box clanked and rattled.

"It sounds broke!" the big man said.

"Most likely, sir!" the deliveryman chirped. "But I'll bet it was something nice!"

The delivery guy pulled out a pencil. "Now…if you'll just sign these damage forms," he said. He waved a huge wad of papers in front of the big man.

"Just sign these five places here."

The deliveryman flipped through the pages quickly. The big man's head spun. He couldn't keep up.

"Oh, yes…print your name here, here, and

of course…here!" the delivery guy said. Then he handed the big man the pencil.

As the burly man began to sign all the forms, the delivery guy looked down at the dog. The pooch was wagging its little tail and blinking its button eyes. Then the dog sat up on its hind legs. Its front paws waved a greeting to the deliveryman.

"Sayyyyyy! That's a mighty cute dog you have there. You don't mind if I pet him, do you, sir?"

"I don't care what you do," the man mumbled. He was busy signing page after page.

The HDS man bent down and took the dog into his arms. "Oo jaa boo ba daa boo boo do booo!" he cooed at the little dog.

"Oh, brother," the big man said to himself as he signed even more pages.

Before the big man could finish, the deliveryman stood up and grabbed the papers.

"That's fine, sir," said the HDS guy, scratching his potbelly, which suddenly seemed a little bigger. "I'll finish these. You have a really nice day now! Bye-bye!"

The HDS man turned and rushed down the hall to the elevator. The big man slammed the door and sat down in front of his big TV screen. He watched it for a couple of minutes, then noticed the dog still waiting by the door.

"Hey, you stupid mutt! Get away from that door!" he yelled. "You ain't gettin' out!"

But the little pooch just sat there.

Really angry now, the big man got up. He went over to the dog.

"Didn't you hear me? *Move!*"

But when the big man bent down to pick up the pooch, he got a real surprise. Instead of a fluffy little dog, he picked up a stuffed animal!

The phony dog wore a collar around its neck. Attached to the collar was a little card. The card read: *You have been had by ACE VENTURA—PET DETECTIVE.*

In a rage, the big man threw the stuffed dog across the room.

"I'm gonna kill that phony HDS guy!" the big man shouted. He grabbed his baseball bat and ran out the door.

2

Batter Up!

The delivery guy was already outside. He hurried down the crowded street.

"Handy Delivery Service coming through!" he called as he weaved around people.

"Excuse me, ladies...big delivery!" he said as he went by two older women.

"Will you look at that!" one of the ladies said, pointing.

"Why, that man's stomach is *moving!*" the other lady declared.

Indeed, it was. The HDS man's potbelly was moving upward. Up and up the lump went. Then his shirt popped open at the neck. A little dog's head peeked out.

"Aroowwwl," the pooch whimpered. The delivery guy reached down and patted the dog. With a voice like a sports announcer, he chattered to the little pooch.

"That was a close one, ladies and gentlemen. But the champ pulled it off!"

"Arf, arf!" barked the dog.

"That's right!" the delivery guy said to his new friend. "I couldn't agree with you more. Unfortunately, every game has a loser."

He stopped and pulled the dog out of his shirt. He held the pooch with one hand as he pointed with the other.

"I"—he pointed at himself—"am the winner. Back there"—he pointed to the apartment building he'd just left—"is the loser. The *looohoooserrrherrr!"*

Ace had stopped before a battered, rusty old car. The Chevy Bel Air used to be blue. Now it was so dirty it was hard to tell what color it was.

The man got out his keys. He unlocked the door and set the dog down on the passenger seat. He took off his HDS cap and threw it in the back. Then he got in himself.

He looked down at the little dog.

"Hi!" he said. "The name's Ventura...Ace Ventura, pet detective. I'm here to take you home to your mommy. Do you want to see your mommy?" Ace Ventura asked.

"*Arf, arf,*" the dog answered. He wagged his tail excitedly.

"Sure you do," Ace said with a wink.

"*Arf! Arf, arf, arf!*" the little dog replied.

"What's that? Are you hungry, fella?"

Ace pulled open the car's ashtray. It was filled with tasty puppy food. "There you go. Eat up while I get us out of here."

Ace Ventura turned the ignition key and stepped on the gas. The car's engine chugged once, but did not start. The dog stopped eating and looked at Ace.

"Now take it easy, big fella," the pet detective said, shaking his head. "It's no problem. The engine gets a little flooded now and then. We'll just give it a minute."

Ace Ventura sat back and looked out the windshield.

Suddenly he sat up straight. "On the other hand, maybe I should try it now!" he cried.

Standing outside of the car was the big burly man! In his hand was a very large baseball bat. He raised the bat above his head.

"Ya little creep," the big man howled. "Gimme that dog!"

Smash!

The windshield broke as the bat landed.

"Oooh, boy," said Ace.

"Arf!" barked the pooch.

The pet detective ducked low as he turned the key for the second time. Again the engine chugged but did not turn over.

The big man circled the car. He slammed it with the baseball bat several more times. Then he came to Ace's side of the car. The detective could see the big man's face in the side mirror.

"Warning," Ace said, "jerks are closer than they appear."

"Argh!" the big man screamed. He knocked the mirror off with his bat. Then the man ran behind the car. He raised the bat again.

"Excuse me," Ventura wisecracked. "Since you're back there, could you give me a push?"

The man howled and brought the bat down. The back window shattered. Glass sprinkled into the backseat.

"All rightee then!" said Ace.

"Arf, arf, arf!" barked the dog.

"What, you think you can do better?" Ace snapped.

He turned the key again. This time, the engine roared to life.

"It's alive!" Ace shouted. *"It's alive!"*

He slammed the car into gear and spun the wheels. But just before Ace sped away, the big man dropped the bat and dived through the back window.

Ace turned to find the man's beefy hands clutching the back of his seat.

"I'm gonna kill you!" the big man roared.

But before he could do anything, the dog jumped up and bit the big man's hand.

"Ow!" the man shrieked.

"Great idea!" Ace said. He turned his head and bit the big man's other hand.

"Ow!" the big man bellowed.

Ace growled as he dug his teeth in. With a final scream, the man let go. Ace put on the gas as the big man slid out the window. Then Ace turned a corner fast. The man couldn't hold on anymore. He flew off the trunk and landed in the street.

"*Arf!*" the dog barked.

"*Arf! Arf!*" Ace barked back.

The old car sped away. Most of the windows were broken, and there were new dents. But Ace and the pooch were safe at last.

Ace couldn't see through the cracked windshield. So he put on his snazzy sunglasses and stuck his head out the window. The dog stuck his head out the other window.

"*Arf, arf, arf!*" the dog and the detective barked as they sped home.

Later that day, Ace and the little dog stood outside the door of a fancy apartment. Ace was wearing a colorful Hawaiian shirt and had his hair slicked up in his trademark style.

The dog had just had a bath, and his fluffy fur was combed out. A nice blue bow was tied on top of his head.

The dog and the detective both looked extra spiffy. Ace knocked.

The door swung open, and there stood a

beautiful woman. She smiled at Ace.

"*Arf, arf, arf, arf!*" the little dog barked.

"Baby!" the woman cried.

She scooped up the little dog and hugged it as Ace looked on. He nodded to himself. It was a job well done.

"You missed Mommy, didn't you?" the woman cooed. "Did that bad man hurt you? I won't let him near you ever again!"

She kissed the dog and held it close. Then she looked at the pet detective.

"Thank you, Mr. Ventura," she murmured. "How can I ever repay you?"

"Well," Ace said with a big smile, "the reward would be good. There was also some damage to my car. It's a high-performance vehicle, and also quite rare—"

The woman put down the dog and put her arms around Ace's neck.

"How about if I just give you a great big kiss?" she purred.

"Well...*sure!*" said Ace.

"*Arf, arf!*" barked the dog.

The Game's a Fin

Super Bowl season was in full swing at Dolphin Stadium. The Miami Dolphins were playing in the Super Bowl this year, and the big game was only fourteen days away!

In a couple of weeks, the stadium would be filled with cheering people. And two teams would meet on the field. It would be winner take all, with the winning team getting to wear the ring of champions.

On this sunny afternoon, the stands were empty. But the field was not. The Miami Dolphins were practicing. They were running plays as the coach watched.

In a huge water tank on the sidelines, the team mascot was busy too. Snowflake the dolphin was getting ready for the game. His trainer threw him a football. The dolphin caught the ball with his nose, then swam to a goalpost set up at the end of his tank. There, he kicked the ball with his tail. A field goal!

He finished with a victory jump through a hoop.

Snowflake was an important member of the team. He even had his own number—number 4. Snowflake's work came at halftime. While the band played, the dolphin put on a show for the fans. He was the most famous mascot in pro football. The fans all said that Miami couldn't win without Snowflake.

That night, the stadium was completely empty. The only sounds in the darkness came from Snowflake splashing in his tank.

Suddenly, one of the stadium gates rattled open, and a large van drove up to the tank. As the van pulled to a stop, the rear door slid quietly open.

Two men wearing black wetsuits jumped out and, with hardly a sound, slipped into the water. A third figure stood off to the side in the shadows. A ring on his finger gleamed in the moonlight.

Snowflake popped his nose above the surface and looked around curiously. Then the dolphin noticed one of the strangers waving a fish in the air.

Snowflake swam over to the man. He blew some water through his breathing hole and opened his mouth. Then the dolphin leaped up and bit into the snack, leaving only the tail of the fish in the man's hand.

Snowflake circled the tank once, then swam back to the man for more.

But suddenly, Snowflake was feeling *very* sleepy. When the two men reached out and grabbed the dolphin, he was too groggy to struggle.

As the strangers dragged him to the edge of the tank, Snowflake slipped into a deep sleep.

With the third figure's help, the strangers lifted the dolphin out of the water and carried him to the van. Inside the van, Snowflake was put into a small water tank. He was still sound asleep.

Their task completed, the three men

jumped into the van and sped off into the night.

The next morning, Ace Ventura parked his battered Bel Air in front of the Surfside Apartments, where he lived. He whipped off his sunglasses and smoothed his ducktail haircut. Then Ace jumped out of the car and lifted two big bags full of pet food.

Carefully, Ace entered the building and passed Mr. Shickadance's apartment. Ace was very quiet. Mr. Shickadance was Ace's landlord and, as usual, Ace was late with the rent.

But just as he put the key into the door of his apartment, Ace heard a raspy, wheezing voice behind him.

"Venturrraaaaa...cough! hack!" went the voice.

Ace straightened up but didn't turn around. Instead, he raised one eyebrow and said, "Yes, evil one?"

Turning around, the pet detective found himself face-to-face with Mr. Shickadance.

The little bald man had a big frown on his face as he glared up at Ace.

"Oh, sorry, Mr. Shickadance. You sounded like...somebody else."

"Cut the wisecracks, Ventura," said Mr. Shickadance. "Didn't you forget something?"

"Is it your birthday?" Ace asked. "All righ-tee then! I'll just bop on down to the flower shop and pick out some nice poison ivy!"

Mr. Shickadance's face turned a bright shade of red as he scowled at the pet detective. He looked as if he was ready to explode.

"You owe me *rent!*" he shouted.

"Gosh, Mr. Shickadance," Ace replied, "you're first on my list. I'm working on a big case right now. Here, look at this!"

The pet detective pulled a piece of paper out of his shirt pocket. The paper had a photograph of a white bird on it and the words $25,000 REWARD in big letters.

"This is a picture of a very rare white pigeon," Ace told his landlord. "Just as soon as I find this bird, you're paid!"

But Mr. Shickadance was not impressed.

He just glared at the pet detective for a moment. Then he said, "I heard animals in your apartment, Ventura. They were scratching around all morning!"

"I never bring my work home with me, sir," Ace replied. Animals were not allowed in the building.

"Oh, yeah?" the landlord said. He pointed to the bags in Ventura's arms. "Then what are all those boxes of pet food for?"

Ace looked down at the two bags in his arms, then back up at his landlord.

"Er…fiber?"

Ace could tell that Mr. Shickadance didn't believe him. He shrugged his shoulders and said, "All rightee then! Do you want to take a look for yourself?"

Ace turned and put his key into the lock. He rattled it loudly a few times, then confidently opened the door.

The door swung open to reveal a tidy little three-room apartment. There was a television, a couch, a white refrigerator with magnets all over the door…and not a creature in sight.

Ace stood aside and waved his landlord in. "Go on," Ace said. "Snoop around, tough guy!"

Mr. Shickadance stepped through the door and listened. Except for the ticking of the clock on the wall, the apartment was silent. Mr. Shickadance shook his head in bewilderment, then walked back into the hallway.

"Well," Ace said. "Are you satisfied?"

"Yeah," Mr. Shickadance answered, still shaking his head. "But don't ever let me catch you with an animal in there!"

With that, Mr. Shickadance stormed down the hall.

"Okay, then," Ace said. "Take care now. Bye-bye…"

Ace went inside the apartment and shut the door. "Looosserrr," he muttered to himself.

Ace looked around the quiet apartment as he set the bags down on the couch. He smiled. Then he put his fingers to his lips and let loose with a loud whistle.

The room exploded with animals!

From every corner, from every nook and

cranny, Ace's pets came running to greet him.

A basset hound ran up to Ace and lay at his feet. Two huge parrots landed on each arm. A seal popped out of the toilet. Two penguins waddled out of the kitchen. A big lizard slunk out from under some laundry. A little black-and-white skunk scampered out from under the bed, followed by a spunky raccoon. A monkey jumped out of the bread box. A tiny baby squirrel with a puffy tail emerged from a can of peanuts.

They swarmed and scampered, they jumped and flew, all of them to the pet detective. They were as happy to see him as they could be. And Ace Ventura was happy too!

Ace fell to his knees to greet his beloved pets. "Come to me, my jungle friends!" he cried. "Ooshooboobooboodoodoo!"

4

Ace on the Case!

Things were pretty glum at Miami Dolphins headquarters. Everyone had heard the terrible news. When the trainer had gone to feed Snowflake that morning, he'd found the tank empty.

The police were called at once. Several officers walked around the tank. They took pictures. Then they had the water drained from the tank.

When that was done, the police searched for clues. The only thing they found was the tail of a small fish. Left over from one of Snowflake's lunches, the trainer said. When no other clues turned up, the police went to talk to the owner of the Miami Dolphins, Don Riddle.

Mr. Riddle ordered the police to keep Snowflake's disappearance a secret. Everyone would be upset, he said. He didn't want the press to find out, either.

Later that day, Mr. Riddle held a small meeting with his two most important employees.

"How do you lose a five-hundred-pound fish?" Riddle asked.

"It's not a fish, sir," said Melissa Robinson. She was Mr. Riddle's young assistant.

"Thank you very much, Ms. Jacques Cousteau," Riddle barked. He was too mad to be polite, even to Melissa.

"How are we going to win this game without Snowflake?" Riddle continued. "Everybody on the team loves that dolphin. The fans love him too. That fish is a valuable member of the team!"

Mr. Riddle turned and pointed to his assistant coach, Roger Podacter. "Keep this a secret. We can't let the public know about this yet."

Roger Podacter swallowed hard, then nodded. "Yes, sir!" he replied smartly.

"Now get out of here," Riddle ordered. "Find that fish, or find new jobs!"

After the meeting, Melissa slumped down at her desk. How was she going to locate that dolphin?

Then an older secretary named Martha walked over to Melissa. "When I lost my Cuddles," she said, "I hired a pet detective."

"A what?" Melissa asked. "A *pet* detective?"

"Oh, yes," Martha said. "Pet detection is a very involved and scientific process! The nice detective I hired told me all about it."

Melissa put her pencil to her lips. She ran her hands through her hair. She was thinking about Martha's suggestion.

Then Melissa made up her mind. She turned to Martha. "What was the name of that pet detective?" she asked.

At that moment, Ace Ventura was cooing like a pigeon. In fact, he was acting in every way like a pigeon.

He was perched on a high roof. His head bobbed up and down like a bird. And he flapped his arms as if they were wings, all the while trying not to fall to the alley far below.

The reason for these antics was perched on the opposite side of the peaked roof. There sat the rare white pigeon Ace was searching for.

Ace was slowly closing in on the bird. He walked along the tip of the peaked roof. He took one careful step at a time. After a long and shaky walk, he was finally in reach of the bird.

The white pigeon turned its head to look hard at the strange creature coming toward it.

"*Coo, coo,*" Ace said as he inched closer to the pigeon.

The pigeon's head bobbed up and down. Ace's head bobbed up and down. Then the bird spread its wings. Ace spread his arms. Then the bird jumped into the air. Ace jumped into the air after it…right off the edge of the roof!

"*Aaaaaaah!*"

Down Ace plunged to the alley below. Surprisingly, he had a very soft landing.

"Whew," Ace said in relief. Then he smelled the air around him.

"Ugh!" Ace said, grimacing as he smelled what had broken his fall: a huge pile of fresh—and not so fresh—garbage.

Just then, Ace heard his beeper go off in his pocket.

Martha poked her head into Melissa Robinson's office at Dolphins headquarters. "Mr. Ventura is here to see you," she said.

Melissa rose from her desk. "Okay, send him in."

Ace walked into the room wearing his special business meeting clothes. He still wore his favorite Hawaiian shirt, but he'd added a spiffy pair of baggy pin-striped pants.

Ace pulled off his snazzy sunglasses and reached out to shake Melissa's hand.

"I'm glad you got my message, Mr. Ventura," she said, eyeballing the pet detective's strange appearance. "Please sit down."

Ace leaned back in his chair and made himself at home. Melissa crossed the room and put a tape into the VCR. Then she turned the television on. The screen showed Snowflake catching a football and kicking a field goal.

"Last night," Melissa told the detective, "our team mascot was stolen from his tank. His name is Snowflake, and he's a bottlenose dolphin."

While he watched, Ace pulled a handful of sunflower seeds from his pocket and began to chew on them. His front teeth munched like a squirrel. He spit the shells into his hands. Then he placed them in a little pile on Melissa's desk.

When she saw this, Melissa asked the pet detective if he wanted an ashtray.

"No, thanks," Ace replied. "I don't smoke. It's a disgusting habit." He continued to munch away.

"I have to be honest," Melissa said. "Before Martha told me about you, I didn't even know there was such a thing as a pet detective."

"Well," Ace replied, "now you know who to call if your schnauzer ever runs away."

Amazed, Melissa blurted out, "How did you know I have a schnauzer?"

Ace reached out and pulled a tiny strand of hair from her blouse. He looked at the hair closely.

"I'd say he's young, weighs about five pounds, has a black coat with white speckles, and"—Ace sniffed the hair carefully—"he likes to chase cars."

Melissa nodded. "I'm impressed, Mr. Ventura. You were right on all counts."

She paused, then said, "Mr. Ventura, I think you're the right man for the job. Do you think you can find Snowflake?"

"Well," Ace pondered. "Sea creatures aren't really my specialty…"

"We'll pay you five thousand dollars if you find Snowflake before Super Bowl Sunday."

Ace Ventura sat up straight. He thought about the money he owed Mr. Shickadance, and the rising price of pet food.

"You've got yourself a deal, Ms. Robinson!" Ace said, smiling his goofy smile.

Melissa took the pet detective down to the field. The team was running plays and practicing for the game. Melissa showed Ace the empty dolphin tank.

"So," he said as he looked down at the bottom of the empty pool. "Did the police make you drain this tank?"

"That's right."

"And what's this?" Ace asked as he picked up the tail end of a little fish. He sniffed it once.

Melissa wrinkled her nose. "I guess it's part of Snowflake's supper," she answered.

"Wrong!" Ace cried. "The smell of this tail fin tells me it was a *Mickey* tail-Finn!"

"A *what!*" Melissa gasped.

"A Mickey Finn is the name for a drugged food or drink," Ace replied in his detective voice. "This fish was pumped full of a powerful drug. When Snowflake ate it, it put him to sleep. That's how the thief got the dolphin out without alerting the guards."

Ace threw the fish tail to the ground. "This was a very professional job," he said. Then he turned and looked down into the water tank.

31

"I'm going down there," he announced. "If I'm not back in five minutes…wait longer."

With that, Ace climbed down the ladder and into the tank. He walked around inside the huge container. His footsteps echoed eerily off the walls. He leaned down and sniffed the corners. He prodded the walls. He circled around and around.

Melissa watched him until she heard a crowd of people that sounded like they were coming closer.

"Oh, no," Melissa said to herself. A large group of reporters with television cameras were in the stadium. And they were coming her way!

She looked down into the tank.

"Ace," she called. "Ace! Get out of the tank! Hurry! The press is coming. We don't want them to know about Snowflake."

But Ace ignored her. He continued to search the tank. He stuck his hand into a large drainpipe and felt around. He grimaced as he pulled out a handful of slime. Then he reached back in.

"Hmm," Ace said as he felt a small, hard object. His fingers closed around it, and he pulled it out. He wiped the slime off it and discovered a tiny amber gemstone.

"Ace!" Melissa begged. "Please get out of there!"

Then Melissa ran over to head off the reporters. Ace carefully climbed up the ladder. When he got to the top, he saw Melissa talking to the members of the press.

"So, where's Snowflake?" asked one guy with a camera. "I'm supposed to get a shot of his new trick for the evening news."

"What do I do now?" Melissa moaned to herself.

5

Ace Sniffs Out Some Suspects

"Yeah," another reporter said. "Where's Snowflake?"

"Nothing happened to him, I hope," said another.

A third reporter looked at Melissa suspiciously. "I think you're hiding something," he said. "What happened to the dolphin?"

Poor Melissa felt trapped. She didn't know what to do. All the reporters were looking at her. She could tell they suspected something was wrong. And she wasn't allowed to tell them the truth.

"Vell!" interrupted a loud voice from the top of the tank. Everyone looked up.

There was Ace Ventura. He waved his arms dramatically.

"Und vat do ve have here?" Ace asked in a crazy German accent. "How can I be getting

34

dis work done mit all der shouting? Vat for is dis shouting?"

The reporters were dumbfounded.

"Who is that?" one of them finally asked.

"And what is he saying?" blurted another.

"Uh, why that's, uh…" Melissa stumbled.

"Heinz Kissvelvet ist who I am!" Ace jumped in. "I am der trainer of der dolphin. You vant to talk to ze dolphin, you talk to me *first!*"

Now Ace had everyone's attention. He jumped down from the tank. With a wave of his hand he addressed the crowd of reporters.

"Vy do you care about ze dolphin?" Ace bellowed. He walked up to one reporter and looked him in the eye.

"Are you a friend of der dolphin? Does der dolphin call you at home? *Do you have a dorsal fin?*"

The reporters didn't know what to make of this!

"It is *me* you must speak to! *I* am der artist! Not der dolphin. To train der dolphin, vun must get into der head of der dolphin! Vy, just

35

yesterday, I zay to Snowflake, I zay 'EEEEEEEE! EEEEEEEE! EEEEEEEE!'"

The high-pitched sound made some of the reporters cover their ears. Others began to leave. Soon they were all leaving. The reporters had had enough of Ace Ventura!

"...Und Snowflake zaid to me, 'EEEEEE, EEEEEEurrrppp!' Und you can quote him!" Ace shouted at their backs.

"Thank you, Mr. Ventura!" Melissa said gratefully.

"All in a day's work," the pet detective replied. "And you can call me Ace...Melissa."

Melissa blushed. To cover her embarrassment, she got back to business. "Are you finished looking at the tank?" she asked.

Ace looked down at the amber stone resting in the palm of his hand.

"Oh, yes," he said importantly. "I'm finished."

Later that day, Ace went to the Metro Police Headquarters to see his old pal, a policeman named Emilio. He hoped Emilio could give him the inside scoop on what the police were doing on the Snowflake case.

The squad room at headquarters was busy. Police officers were running back and forth. Telephones were ringing. People were typing. But everyone looked up when Ace Ventura walked through the door.

One cop looked over at his partner and said, "Hey, look, it's the pet detective!"

"Yeah," said the other cop. "Maybe Lassie is missing." They both laughed.

Ace ignored their taunts. That is, until his archenemy, Sergeant Aguado, arrived. Aguado was a big, fat cop who didn't like private detectives very much. Especially *pet* detectives.

"Hey, Ventura," Aguado hollered. "Find Big Bird yet?"

Everyone in the squad room laughed.

"Shhh, everybody," Aguado said. "Maybe Ventura made a good collar...or is that a leash!"

Everybody burst out laughing again. This time, Ace Ventura stopped in his tracks. He bobbed his head in thought. When Ace had made up his mind, he said to himself, "All rightee then!"

Ace turned and faced Aguado. The fat sergeant stared back at Ace. Then Aguado noticed a bug crawling across the floor. He walked over to the bug and crushed it with his foot.

"Uh-oh," Aguado said to Ace. "Looks like a murder, Ventura! How you gonna solve this one?" All the cops laughed again.

"Well, good question, Aguado," the pet detective replied. "First, I'd establish a motive."

Ace rubbed his chin in mock thought. "In this case, I'd say the killer became insanely jealous when he saw the size of the bug's brain!"

Ace smiled his goofy smile at the fat sergeant.

Now Aguado was mad. He balled up his beefy fist and took a swing at Ace.

Quickly, the pet detective sidestepped the punch and grabbed Aguado by the arm. He threw the cop to the floor and held him there.

Aguado's mouth was almost touching the squashed bug.

"Now kiss and make up," Ace said as he let go of the big policeman.

Ace stepped over Aguado, wiped his hands together, and headed over to Emilio's desk. His friend was busily typing away.

"Hi, Emilio!" Ace said. "Is this seat taken?" Ace sat down, flashing a toothy smile.

Emilio stopped typing. He wasn't very happy to see Ace.

"You'd better get out of here, man," Emilio said. "I'd like to chat, but if Lieutenant Einhorn sees you here, there's going to be trouble!"

Just then an ominous shadow fell over Ace. He looked up. A tall woman stood next to Emilio's desk. She had a frown on her face and held her arms tightly folded across her chest.

Emilio jumped out of his seat and stood at attention. "Can I help you, Lieutenant Einhorn?" he blurted.

"Holy Tick-Tock Tuesday!" Ace said, jumping to his feet.

"What is *he* doing here?" asked Lieutenant Lois Einhorn icily. She was staring at the pet detective with hate in her eyes.

"Hello, Lois," Ace said. "Actually, I came to confess. I...I helped the Grinch steal Christmas." Ace hung his head in mock shame.

"Spare me your jokes, Ventura," Einhorn said. "I know you're working on the Snowflake case. Just stay out of it. We'll find the porpoise."

"Whew," Ace said, running his hand across his brow. "Now I feel *much* better."

Ace turned and began to leave. Then he stopped in his tracks.

"Of course," Ace said, his finger raised, "that might not do any good. You see, nobody is missing a *porpoise*. It's a dolphin that's been stolen!"

Lieutenant Einhorn had had enough! "Listen, Ventura," she said angrily. "How would you like me to make your life totally miserable?"

Ace frowned. He got very serious. He stared deeply into Lieutenant Einhorn's eyes.

"Gosh, I'm really not looking for a steady girlfriend right now, Lois. But thank you for asking."

Einhorn just stood there. Ace turned and headed for the exit. At the door, he turned back to the pretty, but scary, police lieutenant.

"Well, maybe I *could* give you a call some-time…is your number still 911?"

"Ventura!" Einhorn shrieked, waving her arms in anger.

But Ace Ventura was already out the door.

That night, Ace was forced to go to one of the most dangerous places in the world.

Shivering with fear, Ace walked down a long, dark alley. Garbage cans lined both sides of the dirty street. Rats scurried around his feet. Finally, Ace came to a door at the end of the alley.

Ace stopped and took a deep breath. Then he squared his shoulders and pushed the door open. What he found inside was total chaos. Destruction. Violence. Madness. Mayhem. And incredibly loud thrash metal music!

Ace had entered the infamous Tea Room, the wildest nightclub in Miami. Inside were hundreds of metal heads. They wore leather jackets and punk haircuts. They danced around wildly to the throbbing beat of the music.

Some were bouncing around in a huge mosh pit at one end of the club. Others were dashing onstage, then leaping into the crowd. Some of them were caught. Others just crashed to the floor.

As he tried to cross the room, Ace kept running into people. And people kept running into him. Soon Ace was helpless in the crush of people.

"Excuse me, excuse me," the pet detective pleaded. The crowd ignored him. Ace was tossed back and forth. He bounced off a wall. He bounced off the floor.

Finally, the worse for wear, Ace made it across the room. He dusted himself off, then went down a secret flight of steps. At the bottom of the stairs was a steel door. Behind this door was a place known only to a very few people.

Ace banged on the door three times. He waited until he heard a voice from inside.

"Password!" the voice demanded.

"New England clam chowder!" Ace called back.

"Is that the red kind or the white kind?" the mysterious voice asked.

Ace looked stricken. "I can never remember this one..." Then he said, "The white kind!"

Ace breathed a sigh of relief as the metal door slid open. Inside was the secret headquarters of his pal Woodstock—friend to endangered species everywhere. Around the room were banks of computers. Television screens flickered with pictures and data. Wires crisscrossed the floor. Tapes whirled and printers printed.

In the center of it all stood Woodstock. Woodstock was a tall, thin man with long gray hair. He wore a fringe jacket and a headband with a peace sign on it. Woodstock also wore big, puffy bellbottom blue jeans and two different pairs of glasses—one in front of the other.

"Hey, Woodstock!" Ace said.

"Hey, man," Woodstock replied. "How's it going, dude?"

"Super, and thank you very much for asking," Ace answered.

Woodstock took a seat in front of a large computer screen. The screen was black, except for little white electronic blips.

"What's going on?" Ace asked when he saw the screen.

"I'm watching the fishes, man," Woodstock said. "You see those blips?"

"Yeah," Ace replied.

"That's the Norwegian whaling fleet. I'm sending them false information. They'll find the Wizard of Oz before they find any whales!"

"Groovy," Ace said, impressed.

"So what can I do for you?" Woodstock asked, turning to the pet detective.

Ace sat down next to Woodstock. "Can

44

you still access all the aquatic supply stores in the city with your computer?"

"Sure can, dude," the ex-hippie said. "Why?"

"I want to trace the sale of any equipment for moving or keeping a dolphin, say in the last two or three weeks."

Woodstock looked disappointed. "Gee, man," he said, "I thought you had a challenge for me!"

Woodstock turned to his keyboard and started typing away. The man continued working for a few minutes. While he waited, Ace ate a few sunflower seeds. Finally, Woodstock spoke.

"Got something!" Woodstock said. "This is a lot of equipment for a civilian to buy…"

Ace looked over his friend's shoulder at the computer screen. The pet detective was surprised at what Woodstock had found. On the screen was the picture of a very famous man in Miami.

"Ronald Camp? The billionaire?" Ace said in amazement.

"Billionaire *and* rare fish collector," Woodstock added. "This guy is always trying to get his hands on endangered species."

Woodstock pressed a few more keys. Another picture of Ronald Camp appeared. This time the billionaire was standing beside the Miami Dolphins football team!

"Wait a minute!" Ace cried. "Does this guy have something to do with the Dolphins?"

"Sure, man," Woodstock answered. "He donated the land that the stadium is built on."

Woodstock hit a few more keys, then pointed to a date on the screen. "And it looks like Mr. Camp is throwing a special Super Bowl party tonight."

"Tonight, eh?" Ace said, rubbing his chin in thought. "Something smells fishy here. I'm going to crash that party! I wonder if I can get a date."

6

Party Animal

That night, Ace Ventura stood with Melissa Robinson in front of Ronald Camp's huge mansion. The billionaire's estate was beautiful. The house itself was made of marble. It was surrounded by spacious gardens, with a swimming pool covering part of the backyard. Palm trees waved gently in the night air.

Long black limousines pulled up front. Women in long gowns and men in tuxedos walked arm in arm up the staircase to the front door.

Melissa looked beautiful. She was wearing a black gown cut low in the back. Around her neck she wore a diamond choker.

Ace, on the other hand, was wearing his usual baggy pants and Hawaiian shirt. But for tonight's special occasion he'd also donned a white evening jacket. As he and Melissa walked up the steps, Melissa lectured the pet detective.

"I'm really taking a chance here, Ventura," Melissa said. "You'd better behave yourself. If you do something stupid, I could lose my job!"

"I sense your nervousness," Ace said as he knocked on the huge door.

"And I swear," Melissa warned, "if you do anything to embarrass me in front of Mr. Camp..."

"You mean like this?" Ace interrupted. He began to make spastic body motions. He flapped his arms and rolled his eyes up into his head.

At that moment, a bald man wearing a white jacket opened the door. Ace continued his act until Melissa swatted him with her purse.

"Owww," Ace squawked.

Then Ace saw the butler. Because the man looked more like a sea captain than a butler, Ace saluted the man and said, "Permission to come aboard, sir!"

The butler rolled his eyes in disgust. Melissa used her purse on Ace again, then stormed through the door. Ace followed.

The party was in full swing. All the most important people in Miami were there. And all of them turned to watch Melissa and her date enter. Ace basked in the attention. He walked by, flashing everyone his goofy smile.

At the other end of the room, Ronald Camp also noticed Melissa's arrival. He was a tall man wearing a black tuxedo. Camp set his drink down and picked up his cane. He walked, with a slight limp, over to Melissa.

"I'm so glad you could make it, Melissa," Ronald Camp said. Then he noticed Ace Ventura. "And who is this?" Camp asked politely.

"This? Oh, this is…my date," Melissa said. "He's a lawyer," she added.

"Does he have a name?" Camp asked smoothly. "Or should I just call him 'Lawyer'?"

Ace Ventura reached out and shook hands with Ronald Camp.

"Ace is my name, Tom Ace…" the pet detective said, pumping Camp's hand. "Wonderful to meet you, Mr. Camp. And congratulations on all your success. Gee, you smell terrific!"

Melissa squirmed uncomfortably. Ronald Camp sniffed himself. Ace continued his banter.

"So, how's everyone feeling tonight? All rightee then!" Ace pointed to a table spread with food. "Look, honey! There's the grub! Let's go…"

Ace grabbed Melissa's arm and pulled her along. She continued to squirm in embarrassment.

"This is crazy," Melissa whispered to Ace. "There's no way Ronald Camp stole Snowflake!"

"Oh, no?" the pet detective asked. "Then why did he buy all that aquatic equipment? Look, you just keep Camp busy, and I'll work my magic."

Ace headed to the refreshment table. He began stuffing his face with anything and everything in sight. When a well-dressed gentleman walked over to the table, Ace greeted him.

"Toooomoeoirolmvgo, emmmph?" said Ace.

"Pardon me?" replied the man. Ace spit some food out of his mouth and repeated his question.

"I said, 'Tasty, isn't it?'"

"Hmph," the man grunted, and walked away.

"Geez, what's wrong with him?" Ace muttered as he continued to gobble up food. When he was finished, Ace checked his watch. Time to set his plan into motion.

Ace sauntered over to Ronald Camp and Melissa, who were talking. Ace tapped the billionaire on the shoulder.

"Excuse me, Mr. Camp," Ace said loudly. "I need to use the bathroom—I'm feeling sort of sick. It must be the food, you know?"

"I'm sorry, Mr. Ace," the billionaire said. "The bathroom is just down that hall."

Ace leaned toward him. He looked

around, then whispered loudly, "The food probably looks better on the way out, huh?"

Camp was dumbfounded. Melissa fidgeted in shame.

"All rightee then!"

And Ace was off. Everything was going according to plan. He quickly found the fancy marble-and-brass bathroom. He closed and locked the door. Then he turned on the tap so that the sound of the water would cover any noise he made. He popped open the small window above the sink and crawled through.

Once outside, Ace jumped to the ground. He was in the garden. Everything was dark. To his left was the pool and a large building which looked like a huge aquarium.

Ace bent low and sneaked through the garden. He climbed the fence by the pool. Then he crept over to the building and swung open the only door. Luckily, it wasn't locked.

Ace slipped inside and shut the door behind him. He was right. This was Ronald Camp's private aquarium. The walls were lined with tanks filled with seawater and hundreds of rare tropical fish. Each tank was eerily lighted. The sound of bubbling and gurgling filled the room.

The detective walked down the corridor. At the end was a very large tank. This one had no windows. A ladder reached to the top.

"Gravy!" Ace muttered to himself.

Ace went to the ladder and began to climb. When he got to the top, he found a narrow catwalk that crossed the length of the tank. The top of the tank was open, and Ace could see deep, dark water. Ace also found a bucket filled with dead fish. He grabbed one of the tasty-looking fish by the tail and stepped onto the walkway.

Ace dangled the fish over the water. "Snowflake...here, Snowflake..." he whispered.

Ace could see bubbles coming from just below the surface. He leaned closer to the water.

"Come and get it, Snowflake...Snow-flake..."

Suddenly the surface of the pool exploded in a shower of foam. A gigantic great white shark lunged out of the tank. Its razor-like teeth snapped shut an inch from the pet detective's startled face!

Ace reeled back—and fell off the other side of the narrow walkway.

Splash!

Gasping for breath, Ace swam for the edge of the tank. "It's n-not Sn-snowflake!" he sputtered. "It's not Snowflake!"

Then Ace felt a tug on his pants leg.

"It's not Snowflake!" the pet detective shouted as the shark grabbed him and began dragging him back and forth across the tank.

Meanwhile, back at the party, a long line had formed outside of the bathroom. Melissa stood nearby with Ronald Camp.

"Do you think your friend is all right?" Camp asked Melissa. "He's been in the bathroom a long time."

"Who, Tom?" Melissa laughed nervously. "I'm sure he's fine."

At that moment, the bathroom door swung open. Out stepped Ace Ventura. Everyone's jaws dropped. Ace was dripping wet. His pants were in tatters from the shark attack. Even his prize Hawaiian shirt was torn.

But the pet detective remained cool. Fanning the air around him dramatically, he shouted, "Do *not* go in there!"

Then, to get the point across, Ace pinched his nose and said, "Phew!"

Ronald Camp grew pale. The butler rushed over to Ace with a towel. And poor Melissa thought she would faint from shame on the spot!

Ace walked over and grabbed Melissa's hand.

"We're leaving," he commanded. Together, they started for the door.

Camp headed them off. "I'm so very sorry, Mr. Ace," Camp gushed. "I—I don't know what could have happened. I'll have the plumbing checked immediately."

Ace turned to face the billionaire. "Be sure that you do," he chided. "If I had been drinking out of that toilet, I might have been killed!"

Camp looked even more confused. He recovered and politely offered Ace his hand.

"Please accept my apologies," Camp said.

When Ace took the man's hand, the detective noticed a unique ring Camp was wearing. When the billionaire tried to release his hand, Ace pulled him closer. The pet detective wanted to get a better look at Camp's ring.

Ace bent Camp's arm up to his face and studied the ring on the billionaire's finger. Camp pulled again, but could not break loose.

"Stop it, Ace!" Melissa cried. She clubbed the pet detective with her purse.

Finally, Ace let go of Camp's hand. The billionaire hurriedly returned to his party as Ace and Melissa rushed off.

Back at Ace's apartment, Melissa let loose with her anger.

"I don't even want to know what happened to your pants!" Melissa shrieked. "You could have cost me my job, you jerk!"

Ace hardly noticed. He was going over the clues in his mind.

"Okay, so I was wrong about Camp. He *is* breaking the law by keeping a great white shark as a pet, but he's not the guy who stole Snowflake." Ace Ventura rubbed his chin in thought. Melissa got madder by the minute.

"First you said he was the guy," she said, "now you say he isn't. I don't understand you!"

Ace reached into his jacket pocket. He pulled out the amber stone that he'd found in Snowflake's tank.

"This," Ace announced, "is the key. So small it was missed by the police. But this is the answer to our twisted little jigsaw puzzle!"

Melissa looked at him doubtfully. "So you found a pebble in Snowflake's tank. Excuse me while I call *60 Minutes*."

"It's not a pebble," Ace said. "It's a rare triangular-cut orange amber." Ace handed the jewel to Melissa. While she examined the stone, Ace crossed the room and pulled a big book off his shelf.

Ace began flipping through the pages. "Tonight I saw the exact same stone in Ronald Camp's ring," he said.

Now Melissa was more confused than ever. "I thought you said Camp didn't steal Snowflake."

"No, Camp is clean," Ace replied. "His ring wasn't missing a stone. But whoever was in that tank the night Snowflake vanished had a ring just like this!"

Ace threw the open book down in front of Melissa. She picked it up. The book was open to a closeup photograph of a gold ring with a group of orange amber jewels in the center.

"Whoever stole Snowflake wore this exact ring—a 1984 Dolphins AFC championship ring!" Ace announced triumphantly. "I find the ring with the missing stone, I find Snowflake!"

Melissa looked at Ace Ventura with new respect. "How are you going to do that?" she asked.

"Simple…" Ace answered.

7

Ace Hunts for a Ringleader

At least, it *sounded* simple.

The day after Camp's party, Ace went to see Melissa at Dolphins headquarters. She gave him a team photograph of the 1984 Miami Dolphins. Ace deduced that everyone in that photo would have been presented with a ring.

Ace also knew that Don Riddle, Ronald Camp, and the assistant coach, Roger Podacter, had been given rings too. Ace had already eliminated Riddle, Camp, and Podacter.

Now the real work started.

At home, Ace put up the picture of the 1984 team. He planned to cross out each player and coach as he checked their rings.

The first day, Ace visited the team locker room. There he eliminated most of the current Dolphins.

Ace had to check on those players who

now played for other teams, and those who had retired.

It was a dirty job, but someone had to do it. That someone was Ace Ventura, pet detective!

A fancy red sports car raced down the highway. Suddenly the battered blue Bel Air driven by Ace Ventura pulled up alongside it. The Chevy swerved and almost clipped the red sports car.

"Hey, stupid," Ace shouted to the other driver. The big man behind the wheel of the sports car stared at Ace. He was a retired football player and a former Miami Dolphin.

"Yeah?" the big man shouted to Ace. "What do you want?"

"Why don't you learn how to drive that fancy car, bub," Ace replied. "You almost hit me!" With that, Ace swerved again and narrowly missed the sports car.

The big man turned red with anger. Almost as red as his sports car! He shook his fist at the pet detective.

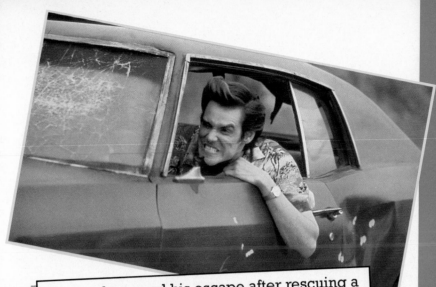

Ace makes good his escape after rescuing a kidnapped dog.

Ace prepares to smuggle pet food past his landlord.

Ace Ventura and his animal friends!

Melissa hires Ace to find the Miami Dolphins' mascot, Snowflake.

Ace investigates the scene of the crime.

Ace grills his police contact, Emilio, for information.

Lt. Einhorn demands that Ace leave the investigation to the police.

Ace escorts Melissa to a party at billionaire
Ronald Camp's mansion.

Ace discovers what Ronald Camp has hidden
in his huge tank—and it's not Snowflake!

Ace returns to the party—soaking wet, but alive.

Ray Finkle's parents welcome Ace to their home.

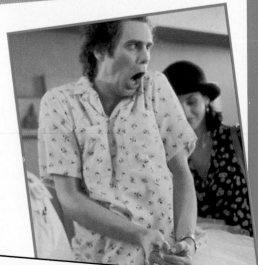

Ace goes undercover to check out the mental hospital from which Ray Finkle escaped.

Ace and Melissa celebrate the successful completion of the case.

Ace produced a pair of binoculars and studied the big man's fist. He was wearing a 1984 championship ring.

To Ace's disappointment, all the amber stones were in place.

The pet detective raced off. The big man gunned his engine and raced after the blue Chevy.

"I'm gonna kill that guy," the big man said to himself.

Later that same day, a bruised and battered Ace Ventura ran down a track. He was chasing another member of the 1984 Miami team. Ace ran and ran, struggling to keep up with the athlete.

But Ace was out of shape. He just couldn't make it. After a few minutes, the pet detective collapsed.

The man ran on.

Big Dan, the quarterback of the Miami Dolphins, was busy entertaining kids at the local orphanage. All the kids were happy to meet

Big Dan. He was a hometown hero.

The kids lined up for Big Dan's autograph. One kid stuck out like a sore thumb. He was twice as tall as the other orphans and wore a goofy smile.

"Hi, Big Dan!" the kid said when it was his turn to get an autographed picture.

"Hi," Big Dan replied. "What's yer name, big fella?"

"My name is Ace," said the tall, goofy-looking kid. When Big Dan signed the picture, the kid bent low and took a close look at his championship ring. All the stones were in place.

"Darn," the kid named Ace said as he left the orphanage. "Another dead end!"

The jogger was back on the track the very next day. He was racing along when he noticed a weird guy in a Hawaiian shirt following him. The big man smiled and put on some speed. He easily dashed ahead of the guy in the goofy shirt.

The weird guy tried to keep up, but soon

fell to the ground. He just couldn't run any-more!

The athlete laughed out loud and ran on.

For the next several days, Ace worked his magic. He hid in a mailbox, waiting for an ex-Dolphin to send a letter. When the man finally did, Ace grabbed his hand and checked the ring. No luck!

Ace got into an arm-wrestling match with another ex-Dolphin. When the man took Ace's little hand in his, the pet detective had just enough time to see that his ring was in perfect condition before the man threw Ace across the room!

Ace landed on a nearby table with a crash. He stumbled home and crossed out another suspect.

Then he went to a local gym where another ex–Miami Dolphin hung out. When the man came into the locker room, Ace was ready. He rolled up a towel and gave the man a loud slap with the wet cloth. Angry, the man turned and punched the pet detective.

When Ace recovered consciousness, he checked his forehead. The imprint of the championship ring was still there. No stones were missing.

Sadly, Ace crossed out another suspect.

Ace continued his quest. Several days later, Ace had crossed off all but one man in the picture.

No more Mr. Nice Guy! Ace thought to himself.

The jogger was taking his usual run around the track. This time, he didn't see the goofy guy in the Hawaiian shirt. Ace ran up alongside the man and stuck out his foot.

The runner tripped over Ace's leg and fell head over heels.

"Sorry!" Ace apologized. He reached down to help the runner up. Shaken from the fall, the man took Ace's hand. The pet detective pulled the huge fist toward him and looked at the man's ring. It wasn't missing any stones.

Ace let go just as the runner was getting

up. The man fell back down again with a grunt.

"Sorry!" Ace Ventura shouted again as he ran to his Bel Air and sped off.

Things looked hopeless to Ace Ventura when he arrived at Melissa's house. He had crossed off every one of the players and coaches in the 1984 team picture. None of them was missing a stone from his championship ring.

It was less than a week before the Super Bowl, and Ace was back to square one!

Melissa led Ace to her backyard. He slumped angrily into a lawn chair. Ace was very depressed. He had never failed before!

"Oh, Ace," Melissa consoled him. "That stone could have come from anywhere...an earring, a necklace..."

Ace glared at Melissa. "It came from a 1984 AFC championship ring," he said menacingly.

"Well," Melissa replied. "Lieutenant Einhorn thinks it was an animal rights group.

Have you ever heard of FAN?"

"Free Animals Now?" Ace snapped. "Started in 1982 by Chelsea Gamble, daughter of the famous millionaire Fisher Gamble? Over half a million members from Florida to Finland? No. Never heard of them."

"Hey," Melissa retorted, "don't get mad at me because you can't figure out this case!"

Ace looked down at Melissa's schnauzer. "What do you feed your dog?"

Melissa was surprised. "Dog food," she answered honestly. "Why?"

"He's miserable."

"What are you talking about?"

Ace pointed to the dog. "Look at him. He's very unhappy. Bad diet, boredom, *your cruelty*. It's amazing he's still alive."

Melissa had heard enough. "You're just mad because your stupid pebble theory didn't work out," she countered. "You are a lousy detective, and you can't deal with failure!"

"Yeah," Ace glowered, "and you're ugly!"

"I'm not even going to talk to you!" Melissa shouted. "Please leave right now!"

"Why? So you can beat this poor defense-less dog?" Ace shouted right back.

Melissa's schnauzer put his head down and covered his eyes with his paws.

Ace looked at the dog and said, "See, he's cowering already."

"Ace Ventura…*you are impossible!*" Melissa yelled. Just then, the phone rang. Still angry, Melissa stalked off to answer it.

Ace looked down at the dog. "You like her, huh?" he asked the schnauzer.

"Arf, arf!" the dog replied.

"Yeah," Ace said, "me too." He got up to apologize to Melissa.

But when Ace entered the house, he found Melissa looking horror-stricken. She was still clutching the phone in one hand. Ace could hear the dial tone.

"Melissa!" Ace cried. "What's wrong?"

Melissa burst into tears. "Roger Podacter is dead!"

8

Murder and a Motive

Police cars, television trucks, and an ambulance were parked in front of a posh high-rise apartment in the center of Miami.

Ace weaved his faded blue Bel Air around the vehicles and parked near the entrance to the building. He and Melissa jumped out and rushed over to the ambulance.

Melissa burst into tears again as she watched the body of Roger Podacter loaded into the emergency vehicle. Then the ambulance drivers closed the doors and drove away.

Twenty floors up, the police swarmed over the apartment of the late assistant coach of the Miami Dolphins. As Ace entered the room, he noticed two police officers he would rather not have seen—Lieutenant Einhorn and Sergeant Aguado. Luckily, Ace's friend Emilio was also there.

"What happened?" Ace asked Emilio.

"It looks like a routine suicide. Podacter jumped. He was alone. There's no sign of a struggle. A neighbor heard him scream on the way down, then rushed in and opened the balcony door. Podacter was already on the ground."

"Did he leave a note?" Melissa asked Emilio.

"No," the policeman replied. "Some do, some don't."

Ace walked over to Podacter's desk. Emilio was right—there wasn't a suicide note. But there *was* an empty file. It looked like all the other files at Dolphins headquarters. But this one was empty. That got Ace's detective radar humming.

The pet detective circled the room. He listened as the neighbor made his statement.

"I got here a couple minutes after I heard the scream," the neighbor told a policeman. "The place was empty, except for that dog in the other room. Then I opened the balcony door, looked down, and...well..." the man frowned and shrugged his shoulders.

Ace saw Podacter's dog cowering in the corner. He went over to the little mutt and took it in his arms.

"Have a bad night, fella?" Ace said to the now-orphaned pet. "Don't worry, boy...I'll give you a new home." The dog licked Ace's face, then started to growl. A shadow fell across Ace and the dog.

"Soooo," Ace said, "animals *can* sense evil."

"Who let Dr. Dolittle in here?" Lieutenant Einhorn barked angrily.

"Ah, Lieutenant..." Emilio said. "He came in with Ms. Robinson."

"Well this is official *police* business," the lieutenant spat. "We'll let you know if the coroner finds any ticks."

Sergeant Aguado and the other cops snickered at Ace. He smiled smugly back at them.

"All rightee then!" Ace said. "If I were Lieutenant Einhorn, I wouldn't want someone tracing my steps and pointing out my mistakes, either."

"So you think we've made some mistakes," Einhorn returned. "I think it's a simple suicide."

Ace shook his head and walked out onto the balcony. He ran his hand along the railing. Then he looked at his finger. Ace then turned to Einhorn.

"Well, there is plenty of evidence to support your theory," Ace said, smiling. The cops looked knowingly at each other.

"Except," Ace said, "for that spot of blood on the railing!"

Einhorn and Aguado both rushed to the railing. There was, indeed, a spot of blood.

"May I tell you what *I* think happened?" Ace asked his now-interested audience. "All rightee then!"

Ace moved to the center of the balcony. "When Roger Podacter returned home, he wasn't alone. Someone was with him. There was a struggle, and Podacter was thrown over the balcony. He hit his head on the railing on the way down, which explains the blood."

Ace paused for dramatic effect, then continued. "Roger Podacter did *not* commit suicide—he was *murdered!*"

But Lieutenant Einhorn was not convinced. "That's a very entertaining theory," she said to the pet detective. "But we *real* detectives have to worry about a little thing called *evidence!*"

"Well," Ace replied, "there *is* just one more thing." The pet detective pointed to Podacter's neighbor. "You said you heard a scream. You ran in here, opened the balcony door, and looked down."

The neighbor nodded.

"What's your point, Ventura?" Einhorn asked.

"Only this." Ace walked back out onto the balcony. He turned and faced the cops, then tipped his head back and screamed at the top of his lungs. *"Aaaaaaaaaaaaaaahhhhhhhhh…"*

Then Ace slid the balcony door closed. No one in the room could hear him. But they could see that he was still screaming.

Then Ace slid the door open and his scream again filled their ears.

"...*Aaaaaahhhhhhhhhhh!*"

Ace stopped screaming. He smiled his goofy smile. Then he stepped confidently into the apartment. He tapped the balcony door as he walked by.

"This is soundproofed glass," Ace announced. "There is no way the neighbor could have heard Podacter scream if that door was closed!"

Ace pointed an accusing finger at Lieutenant Einhorn. "The scream he heard came from inside this apartment. The murderer closed the balcony door before he left!"

The cops looked stunned.

"*Yesss!*" Ace cried as he did a victory dance in front of everyone. Einhorn and Aguado frowned. Ace Ventura, the pet detective, had made a monkey out of them!

"That was pretty impressive," Melissa said to Ace the next day.

"I know," Ace replied smugly. "I was there, remember?"

Ace and Melissa were working together.

They were searching Podacter's office for some clue to his murder. Ace especially wanted to know what that empty file on Podacter's desk had once held.

"Maybe you should have joined the real police force, Ace," Melissa said.

"I don't do humans," Ace replied casually.

Melissa looked at the pet detective. Ace didn't notice her stare. He was busy opening file drawers and pulling out papers.

"You really love animals, don't you," Melissa asked.

Ace stopped what he was doing. He looked up at the ceiling as he mused. "I feel a kinship with them."

"Is that why you do this?" Melissa asked.

Again Ace paused. After a moment, he said, "Have you ever seen a blind man cry tears of joy because you found the Seeing Eye dog he's had for fifteen years?"

Melissa said nothing. She was afraid Ace was just telling another story. Like the one about being the dolphin trainer. Or the one about being "Tom Ace, the lawyer." Melissa didn't know when to believe—or trust—the crazy pet detective.

Suddenly, Ace's shout interrupted Melissa's thoughts.

"Who the heck is *that?*"

Melissa looked at the picture in Ace's hand. It was another photo of the 1984 Miami Dolphins. It had been filed away in Coach Podacter's desk.

"Who?" Melissa asked.

"Number four!" Ace shouted excitedly.

"Oh," Melissa said. "That's Ray Finkle, the kicker. Don't you know who Ray Finkle is?"

"Noooo," Ace said. "How come he's not in the picture I have?"

"He's the guy who missed the winning field goal in the Super Bowl that year," Melissa told him. "He lost the game. The players and fans were so angry that we took Ray out of the *official* team photograph for that year."

"But he got a ring?" Ace asked, a gleam of victory in his eyes.

Melissa smiled. "Definitely."

"A kicker who loses the game," Ace said, thinking aloud. "A kicker who gets thrown off the team, whose number is given to a *dolphin* who can kick a *field goal!*"

Melissa stared at him. She knew what he was getting at.

"All rightee then! Now we have a guy with a ring—and a very big motive!"

A few hours later, Ace arrived in Collier County, Florida. It was a small rural area in the middle of the Everglades. It was also Ray Finkle's hometown.

Ace knew he was there when he saw a large billboard along the road that read: WEL-COME TO COLLIER COUNTY, THE HOME OF MIAMI DOLPHINS KICKER RAY FINKLE.

But the "F" in "Finkle" had been crossed out, and the letters "ST" painted over it. Now instead of "Finkle," the sign read "Stinkle."

"Poor Ray Stinkle—er, Finkle," Ace said to himself.

Ace had already learned a lot about Ray Finkle, but he wanted to learn more. Like, where was Ray Finkle the night Snowflake was abducted? And where was he the night Roger Podacter was murdered?

Before long, Ace came to a little wooden house. The house had once been white. But, like Ace's car, it hadn't been painted in a long time. The house was covered with graffiti. Things like RAY FINKLE STINKS! and GET OUT OF TOWN, LOSER! were scrawled all over the walls in various colors.

Ace parked his Bel Air and got out. He walked cautiously onto the front porch and knocked.

After a few minutes, the front door opened a crack. Ace peeked through the opening, but it was too dark to see anything.

"Hi," Ace said cheerily. "I'm looking for Ray Finkle."

At that, the door opened wider, and Ace found himself staring down the barrel of a loaded shotgun!

9

Ray Finkle's House of Horror

"What do you know about Ray Finkle?" demanded a gruff voice from inside the dark house.

Ace swallowed loudly. Then Ace turned on the charm. He smiled his goofiest smile.

"What do *I* know about *Ray Finkle?*" Ace answered enthusiastically. "Finkle is a southpaw soccer-style kicker. He holds two NCAA Division One records—one for the most points per season, one for distance. The first and only pro athlete to ever come out of Collier County."

Ace swallowed hard again. "And one heck of a model American," he added quickly.

He was relieved to see the shotgun barrel withdraw. The door opened a little wider.

Inside stood an old man with a sour expression. He still held the shotgun. Next to him was a little old lady with gray hair. She eyed the pet detective warily.

"Are you one of them guys from *Hard Copy*?" she asked.

"No, ma'am," Ace answered. "I'm just...a big fan of Ray's. This place is my Graceland."

"Bah!" croaked the old man. He turned his back on Ace and walked away. The little old lady held out her hand.

"It's so nice to meet you," she said. "I'm Ray's mother. You've already met Ray's father."

"Sure have. Nice gun," Ace replied. "It's a real honor, Mrs. Finkle." Ace shook her hand.

"My Ray is really happy to meet his fans," Mrs. Finkle said. "He'll be so pleased you stopped by. Why, he should be home any minute!"

Mrs. Finkle led Ace to her kitchen. She offered him a seat. "Would you like some cookies? I just baked them."

"Wow!" Ace gushed. "Ray Finkle's house! I can't wait to meet him!"

"He ain't comin' home!" Mr. Finkle shouted from the living room.

Ace went into the living room. "Gee, Mr. Finkle," he said. "Your wife says he'll be here any minute!"

"Mrs. Finkle is a lot like Ray," the old man said gruffly. He pointed to his head. "The engine is running, but there's no one behind the wheel."

"Oh, I get it," Ace said perkily. "The clock's ticking, but she's not telling time."

Mr. Finkle ignored Ace and went on. "Eight years ago our son Ray escaped from the Shady Acres Mental Hospital in Tampa," the old man said sadly. "Those doctors couldn't help him. They still bug us to come and pick up Ray's stuff."

Mrs. Finkle came in and offered Ace some cookies. They were shaped like little footballs. And they were still warm.

"It was all Big Dan's fault," Mrs. Finkle said sweetly. "If Big Dan had held the football right, our son would never have missed that kick. Big Dan should have held the football laces out!"

The old lady looked at Ace. "I kept Ray's

room for him," she said, looking upstairs. "When Ray starts kicking again, he'll find his room just like he left it."

"Golly," Ace gushed again. "Could I see Ray Finkle's room?"

"Why, certainly, young man," she replied.

Mrs. Finkle turned the rusty key in the old lock. With a loud click, the door creaked open. Ace stepped inside and turned on the light.

Immediately, he felt goose bumps run down his back. A giant poster of Big Dan, the Miami quarterback, was tacked to the wall. But across the chest of this paper Dan were scrawled the words DIE, DAN, DIE!

In fact, there were words written in red paint—at least, Ace *hoped* it was red paint!—all over the walls. MUST KILL BIG DAN! BIG DAN MUST DIE! and I WILL GET BIG DAN! were just a sampling of what was written on Ray Finkle's walls. Ace shuddered in horror.

"Ray's quite a sports nut, eh?" Mrs. Finkle said.

"He certainly is *nuts*," Ace replied. Then the pet detective saw a newspaper clipping tacked above the desk. He looked closer. SNOWFLAKE THE DOLPHIN GIVEN RAY FINKLE'S OLD NUMBER, the headline read.

"They gave Snowflake Ray Finkle's old number," Ace said to himself. "And then they taught Snowflake how to kick a field goal." Ace shook his head sadly. "Poor Ray Finkle. No wonder he went nuts."

Everything made perfect sense to Ace. Ray Finkle was his man!

Melissa was sitting at her desk at Miami Dolphins headquarters when the phone rang.

"Ace," she cried when she heard the pet detective's voice. "Where are you?"

"I'm in psychoville, and Ray Finkle is the mayor," Ace answered quickly. "Where's Big Dan right now?"

"Why do you want to know about Big Dan?" Melissa asked, puzzled.

"Because he's about to join Snowflake!" Ace warned. "Ray blames Big Dan for his troubles. He's going to kidnap Big Dan before the Super Bowl—I'm sure of it!"

"Oh, my gosh!" Melissa said. "Let me see." Melissa flipped through Big Dan's appointment book. "He's at the Bogart Sound Stage out on Route One," Melissa said quickly.

"Great," Ace said. "I can be there in fifteen minutes. You call the police and get some extra security on Big Dan right now!"

But it was too late. When Ace arrived at the Bogart Sound Stage twelve minutes later, he heard the bad news. Big Dan was already missing.

Witnesses said Dan was last seen with two large guys hired as extras for the commercial Dan was making. They were dressed as football players.

Ace felt terrible. He had let the Miami Dolphins down. He had let Melissa down. And worst of all, now he had to find a missing *human!*

Ace hated to do humans.

*   *   *

"Melissa! Melissa! Wake up!"

Ace Ventura's loud shouting, and his pounding on the door, awakened Melissa from a deep sleep. She got up groggily and put on a robe. Melissa's schnauzer was barking as she stumbled to the door, still only half awake.

"What do you want, Ace?" she asked sleepily as she swung open the door.

"Melissa...this is important." Ace was looking deep into Melissa's eyes.

She was instantly awake now. "What is it?" she asked anxiously. "What's wrong?"

"You have to commit me to the Shady Acres Mental Hospital in Tampa," Ace announced calmly.

10

Ace Goes Off the Deep End

Melissa waited nervously for the doctor at the Shady Acres Mental Hospital to see her. She fidgeted in her seat and thought back to the night before, when Ace had convinced her to go along with his crazy plan.

"Look, Melissa," Ace had told her. "I've got to get into that hospital. Ray Finkle's stuff is still there—there's gotta be a clue!"

Melissa hadn't been entirely convinced last night. Ace's plan sounded even stupider today. But at least the pet detective was acting the part. Ace certainly looked and acted like a crazy person!

"Ms. Robinson?" A kind voice interrupted Melissa's thoughts. "I'm Dr. Handly."

Melissa stood and shook hands with an older man dressed in a white coat.

"Hello, Doctor," Melissa said. "I'd like you

to take a look at my...brother. His name is Eugene."

Melissa pointed across the waiting room. Dr. Handly turned and saw Eugene. His jaw dropped open in surprise.

Ace was dressed in pajamas and was wearing a ballet tutu. On his feet were big, clunky combat boots. His hair was sticking out on all sides. Ace really did look crazy!

As if on cue, Ace jumped to his feet and shouted at the top of his lungs. "I'm ready to go in, Coach," Ace howled. "Just give me the chance!"

Ace struck a dramatic pose, then danced around in a circle.

The doctor turned back to Melissa with a puzzled look. "How long has Eugene been acting like this?" the doctor asked.

"Ohhh, for as long as I've known him," Melissa said truthfully.

Dr. Handly led Melissa on a tour of the hospital. As they walked around the halls, Ace followed behind them.

Ace continued to act crazy. He ran back

and forth, screaming, "I'm open! I'm open!" He jumped up and down. He caught imaginary footballs and ran imaginary touchdowns. He even spiked imaginary footballs.

"He *does* have trouble letting go of the game," the doctor commented. Melissa nodded in agreement.

"I want a new contract, Coach!" Ace howled. "Thirty million over three years, or I'm walking!"

"I want you to know, Ms. Robinson," the doctor told Melissa. "Your brother won't be the first professional football player we've treated."

Melissa nodded.

"Here at Shady Acres we are very sensitive to the emotional stress athletes have to endure."

"Come on, Coach!" Ace screamed. "Let *me* run with the ball…*let me run with the ball!*"

"Are you sure he's not dangerous?" the doctor asked.

"Oh, no," Melissa answered. "He's really quite gentle."

"Well, then, I think your brother will fit in nicely here, Ms. Robinson."

As they walked through the halls, Dr. Handly pointed out areas of interest. They went past the arts and crafts room and the therapy rooms. But Ace's ears really perked up when Dr. Handly mentioned they were passing the storage area. Ace noticed a water fountain right next to the storage room door.

Now that he was where he wanted to be, Ace put a halt to the tour. The pet detective whistled loudly and shouted "Halftime!"

Ace ran in a circle three times. Then he stuck his head in the water fountain and turned the water on. After his hair was dripping wet, Ace sat down on a nearby bench and pretended he was asleep.

The doctor looked curiously at Melissa.

"He thinks it's halftime," she explained. "He won't move for at least twenty minutes."

"Oh," said Dr. Handly, relieved. "Then perhaps you would like to go to my office and talk about your brother's condition?"

"Certainly," Melissa said as she and the

doctor walked down the hall.

Ace was finally alone. Now it was time for him to work the old pet detective magic!

Pulling a wire from his pocket, Ace rushed over to the storage room door. He stuck the wire into the keyhole and jiggled it a few times.

After a minute or so he was rewarded with a loud click. "Yessss," he whispered to himself. Ace opened the storage room door and ducked inside.

The room was cluttered with cardboard boxes. Luckily, the boxes were stacked in alphabetical order. Ace had no trouble locating the cardboard box marked FINKLE, RAY.

Ace pulled the box down and opened it. Inside he found some old clothes. There were also two little portraits that Finkle had painted. Both were crude drawings of Big Dan. One picture had pins stuck in it. The other said BIG DAN MUST DIE across the bottom.

"Obsess much?" Ace said to himself.

He kept rummaging through the box.

There wasn't much else. The pet detective was about to quit when he noticed an old newspaper lying at the bottom of the box.

On the front page was a story that grabbed Ace's attention. The story was circled in red ink. Under the headline SEARCH CALLED OFF FOR MISSING HIKER was a short article. Ace read it with growing alarm.

"A massive search ended today when rescue workers were unable to find the body of Lois Einhorn, a camper reported lost since Friday..."

"Lois Einhorn?" Ace said aloud. "Ray Finkle and Lieutenant Einhorn! Holy butterball turkey! They must be in this together!"

Ace repacked the box. But he stuck the newspaper story in his pocket. Then he threw the box back on top of the stack and crept out of the storage room.

When Dr. Handly and Melissa returned to the bench a little later, Ace was sitting there quietly. When he saw Melissa, Ace jumped to his feet.

"I'm ready for the big play, Coach!" Ace

shouted. "We'll win this one for the Gip-
per…and the next one for Flipper! I can't
wait to do that ESPN special!"

Melissa thanked the doctor for his help.

"Don't you want your brother to begin care
immediately?" Dr. Handly asked.

"Oh, no, Dr. Handly," Melissa replied.
"The season isn't over yet. He has a big game
tomorrow…his teammates are counting on
him!"

Melissa and Ace left poor Dr. Handly
scratching his head. When they got to
Melissa's car, Ace told her about the strange
new clue.

"Einhorn has got to be involved in this,"
Ace told Melissa. "This article is dated the
day before Ray Finkle disappeared from
Shady Acres Hospital!"

"But how is Einhorn involved?" Melissa
wondered.

"I only wish I knew," Ace answered.

"Well," Melissa said after a moment of
silence. "You're quite the dirty rotten liar!"

"You mean my Oscar-worthy performance

back there?" Ace said proudly.

Ace began to mimic an Academy Award winner's speech. "I want to thank everyone connected with this film. You love me, you really love me!"

Melissa laughed. "Where to, Ace?"

"Home, Melissa," Ace said. His tone was serious. "I have a lot of thinking to do."

Back home, Ace gathered his troops around him.

"Snuggles," Ace instructed his pet raccoon. "Get my files out of the closet...but *only* the photo files." Snuggles scurried off.

"Bingo!" A calico cat nearby perked up. "Grab that picture of Ray Finkle on the desk."

"Meow," and Bingo was off.

"Spike," Ace commanded his pet monkey. "I want you to check my newspaper files for any reference to Lieutenant Lois Einhorn."

Chattering, the monkey ran off to the pile of newspapers in the kitchen.

"Arf, arf!" Ace's basset hound barked.

"Sorry, Pepper," Ace told the dog. "You

can't be trusted near newspapers. You remember what happened last time?"

The basset hound hung his head in shame.

"Don't worry, Pepper," Ace told the dog. "I'll have something for you later!"

"Rondo," Ace told the squirrel nearest him, "grab my *National Enquirer* files...and take Boris with you!" Another squirrel joined the first. Soon Rondo and Boris were dragging tabloid papers out of the closet and placing them at the pet detective's feet.

Absent-mindedly, Ace tossed the squirrels nuts. His outstanding—if weird—mind was already working. As always, so was his mouth!

"All rightee then!" Ace said to no one in particular. "The answer has got to be right here! Just gotta get some blood to the brain."

Ace slapped the side of his head a few times. Then he put his chin in his hand and muttered to himself, "Finkle and Einhorn... Einhorn and Finkle. In it together...But how?"

Ace picked up a photograph of Ray Finkle and stared at it. "Finkle and Einhorn... Einhorn and Finkle..." Ace repeated the phrase over and over. But he was still nowhere near a solution.

Hours passed.

Most of Ace's pets had given up and gone to bed. But Ace and Spike the monkey were still at it.

"Finkle and Einhorn...Einhorn and Finkle...Finkle and Einhorn...," Ace said over and over again, until Spike put his paws over his tiny ears.

Ace stared at Spike. The monkey finally gave up. It turned over and was soon sleeping soundly.

"Quitter," Ace said. The monkey snored loudly.

It was then that Roger Podacter's dog came up to Ace. The dog was whimpering. It was trying to get Ace's attention. Finally the pet detective noticed.

"What's the matter, boy?" Ace said to the dog. The little dog ran in a circle and lay at Ace's feet. As it did, the dog's long fur draped over the photograph of Ray Finkle on the floor. When Ace glanced at the photo, it looked as if Ray Finkle had a woman's long hair.

Ace did a double take. He couldn't believe his eyes. He picked up the picture of Finkle and grabbed a pen. He began to draw long hair on the photo—hair just like that worn by Lieutenant Lois Einhorn!

"I can't believe it!" Ace shouted. All the animals perked up. "I've solved the mystery! I've solved the mystery!"

Ace did a bizarre victory dance in the middle of the room. All the animals joined in. Soon the room was a chaos of jumping and scampering creatures. And at the center of the crazy zoo stood Ace Ventura, pet detective, in all his glory!

"Ray Finkle *is* Lois Einhorn!" he shouted. "Lois Einhorn *is* Ray Finkle!"

Then Ace made a mad dash for the telephone. He had to call Melissa!

11

Ace Breaks the Case

Melissa sat in the executive lounge at the football stadium. She was with Don Riddle, the owner of the Miami Dolphins. Emilio, Ace's policeman friend, was also there. He was in uniform. His job was to provide security.

Things were pretty glum. Don Riddle was angry. Melissa was sick with worry. According to the newspapers and television sports shows, Miami fans were pretty down too.

In less than three hours, the Super Bowl was scheduled to begin. If Ace couldn't finish the job in time, then Miami would lose the big game. How could they win? Without Snowflake and Big Dan, the Miami Dolphins were sunk.

And just where is Ace Ventura? Melissa wondered. She had heard from him early that morning. He had claimed he'd solved the mystery. He had told her he knew how and why Lois Einhorn and Ray Finkle were connected.

When she asked him what he'd learned and what he was going to do next, Ace had been secretive. He'd told Melissa it was too dangerous to talk about it over the phone.

Just before he hung up, Ace had promised Melissa that he would have both Snowflake and Big Dan at the stadium in time for the game's starting gun.

But that had been hours ago. And still there was no word from the pet detective. Melissa looked at Emilio. The policeman shrugged his shoulders and shook his head.

Melissa's and Emilio's thoughts were the same. *Where, oh, where is Ace Ventura?*

At that moment, the intrepid pet detective was sitting in his battered blue Chevy Bel Air. He was chewing pack after pack of gum. With a pair of binoculars, he was keeping an eye on an apartment building in one of the nicer sections of Miami. It was an address given to him that morning by Emilio.

Ace had been waiting outside this building for hours. He was getting cranky. He was chewing too much gum. And time was running out.

Ace put another stick of gum into his already overstuffed mouth. Just then, the front door opened. Out stepped the target of Ace's investigation: Lieutenant Lois Einhorn.

She was wearing high heels and a long dress, with her hair down around her shoulders. Ace shuddered. He watched as Lois Einhorn—a.k.a. Ray Finkle—got into a car and pulled out of the parking lot.

Ace turned his ignition key. With a weary cough, the Bel Air started. Ace pulled out of the parking lot right behind Einhorn's car.

Ace followed Einhorn's every move, but was careful to stay a few cars behind. He didn't want Einhorn to spot him. Einhorn weaved in and out of traffic. Ventura followed at a distance.

Soon the traffic grew lighter. They were well outside the city of Miami now. Finally,

Einhorn made a sharp turn off the main road.

Ace slowed down and watched the car as it entered an abandoned dock area by the ocean. There were several large buildings. Some time ago, they were probably factories and warehouses. Now they were rusty, ramshackle hulks waiting to collapse.

Lieutenant Einhorn pulled up to the largest of the buildings and stopped. She got out of her car and walked to a padlocked steel door. She pulled a long key out of her pocket and unlocked the door. Then she went inside.

When Ace thought the coast was clear, he parked his Bel Air well away from Einhorn's car. Then he crept over to the steel door. He pulled on it, but Einhorn had locked the door behind her. Ace couldn't get in.

He would have to find another entrance—and fast!

Inside, Lieutenant Einhorn was talking to her two henchmen. They were the same two goons who had kidnapped Big Dan, and they were still wearing their football uniforms.

"In two hours the Super Bowl starts," Einhorn told the men. "At halftime, we kill the fish. After that, we kill Big Dan!" She began to laugh.

The goons laughed along with her.

Einhorn crossed the empty warehouse. In one corner of the giant complex was a deep pool. Inside the pool, Snowflake swam back and forth. Next to the pool was a large metal support column that reached from the floor to the roof. Tied to that pole was the Miami Dolphins quarterback, Big Dan.

Einhorn walked over to the bound and gagged football player.

"Having fun, Big Dan?" she taunted.

"Moomemmmennffhh!" Big Dan replied.

Einhorn stepped up to the pro quarterback and pulled the gag out of his mouth. He eyed the strange woman who had masterminded his kidnapping.

"Listen, lady," Big Dan said. "I don't know what you think you're doing…"

"I *think* I'm getting my revenge!" Einhorn said.

"Revenge?" Big Dan asked. "Revenge for what? Couldn't you get tickets to the game?"

"Very funny, Big Dan," Einhorn responded. Then she stepped closer to him. She looked Big Dan in the eyes. Big Dan stared back at her.

"Don't you think I look a little familiar?" Einhorn asked. "Don't you feel like you've seen me somewhere before?"

"Lady, I don't know *who* you are or *what* you want!" Big Dan replied.

"You're even stupider than I thought you were, Dan," Einhorn said. She picked up a football and showed it to Big Dan.

"Maybe this will jog your memory," Einhorn said. She placed the ball gently on the ground. She was very careful to turn the laces out. Then she stepped back and squared her shoulders.

With a cry of "Laces out!" Einhorn kicked the ball. It flew high into the air and across the warehouse. Up and up it went, until the ball flew straight through a hole in the roof. In a second it was out of sight.

"Maybe you remember me *now?*" Einhorn cried.

But Big Dan only looked more confused. "Gosh, I don't know," he answered. "I get hit in the head a lot…"

Ace found a ladder to the roof and climbed it. Once on the roof, Ace looked for a way to get inside the warehouse. He searched and searched, but couldn't find an entrance of any kind.

Suddenly, a football sailed out of nowhere and hit him on the back of the head. Ace stumbled around for a few moments, seeing stars, then fell over the edge of the roof!

But, lucky for Ace, he landed after only dropping a few feet. After he shook his head to clear it, Ace found himself lying faceup on a fire escape. And right next to him was an open window.

"All rightee then!" Ace whispered to himself as he crawled through.

Ace found himself in a dark room. He walked cautiously across a dirty floor. Papers and old cans and bottles were strewn about everywhere. Ace was careful not to kick anything that would make a noise and give him away.

Finally, Ace found another door. This one was unlocked. He pulled the door open slowly. The hinges were rusty and squeaked. Ace stepped through the door and into a large hallway. It was then that he heard voices.

He tiptoed down the hall until he found a stairwell with an old metal railing.

When Ace looked over the railing, he knew that the Case of the Missing Mascot was almost closed. Down on the main floor, Ace could see Lois Einhorn, two goons dressed in football uniforms, and Big Dan tied to a pole.

But even more importantly, Ace could see a pool of water in one corner of the warehouse. Swimming in that pool was the missing Miami Dolphins mascot, Snowflake.

Ace allowed himself a smile as he listened to the voices coming from below.

"I'm going into the other room to watch

the Super Bowl pre-game show," Einhorn told her hired goons. "You two morons guard Big Dan and the fish!"

"Yes, ma'am!" the two goons answered in unison. Then Einhorn went through another door and vanished from sight.

This was the chance Ace had been waiting for!

"Hey, Big Dan!" shouted one of the goons. "Watch me throw a pass to the fish."

Snowflake swam to the surface. The big goon threw the football as hard as he could. He threw it so it would *hit* Snowflake, not so the dolphin could catch it.

But the dolphin was too fast. Snowflake dived deep under the surface, and the football hit only water.

"Ha, ha," the other goon laughed. "You missed!"

"Yeah," the first goon said. "But I'll get him next time."

The first goon reached down to get the football, which was still bobbing in the water.

Snowflake saw his chance and took it. The dolphin shot to the surface and whipped his mighty tail fin, creating a huge splash. Both goons were soaked to the skin.

"I'm gonna kill that fish!" the first goon screamed. "Gimme one of those little fish it eats, so I can lure it over here..."

"Duh," said the second goon, holding an empty bucket. "We ain't got no more."

"What do you mean, stupid?" said the first goon. "There's a whole other bucket of fish hanging over there."

The second goon looked around. But there was no bucket.

"I don't see a bucket," he said, confused.

"But I left it right there," the first goon replied. "It was hanging from the ceiling on a long rope."

"Heads up!" Ace Ventura cried from above. "It's naptime!"

When the two goons looked up, Ace let go of the bucket of fish. The bucket hurtled down and bounced off the head of one of the goons with a loud clang.

The goon dropped like a rock.

"Holy cow!" the second goon yelled as he took off running. He headed toward the door as fast as he could go. Ace laughed as he jumped up onto the railing and grabbed the rope.

"All rightee then!" he cried. With an ear-splitting yell like Tarzan's, Ace swung down toward the goon.

Ace's body slammed into the thug, smashing him to the floor. The goon slid across the ground, stopping only when he ran into a wall.

He, too, was out cold.

"Loooo-HOOOOO-seeerrrrrrrrrrr!" Ace cried triumphantly. He let go of the rope and landed gracefully next to Big Dan. He slapped his hands together and said, "All rightee then!"

"Hey," Big Dan asked. "Who the heck are you?"

"Ace Ventura, pet detective," Ace answered. "I don't usually do humans, but I'm making an exception this time. We've got to get out of here—you have a game to win!"

Ace began to untie Big Dan, but he didn't get very far...

"Penalty!" Lois Einhorn shouted, pointing a gun at the pet detective. "Too many men on the field."

Gulp! Ace swallowed hard as he turned and looked down the barrel of Einhorn's pistol.

12

No Way to Treat a Lady

"You should have stayed out of official police business, Ventura!" Einhorn laughed. She waved the gun at Ace Ventura. Her eyes were wild and crazy. "Step away from Big Dan, pet boy!" she ordered.

Ace took two steps back. Then he squared his shoulders and stood his ground.

"You're looking lovely today, Lieutenant Einhorn," Ace said. "Especially for someone who *vanished* in a hiking accident eight years ago!"

"Shut up, Ventura," Einhorn hissed. "You talk too much." The lieutenant reached into her pocket with her free hand and pulled out a cellular phone.

"Careful with that phone," Ace Ventura warned. "I wouldn't want you to get a tumor."

But Lieutenant Einhorn wasn't listening to Ace. "Sergeant Aguado," Einhorn said into the phone. "Get some men over to the old ironworks docks on Victorville Road."

Einhorn smiled meanly and stared at the pet detective. "I've got the kidnapper trapped in the warehouse. It's Ace Ventura, the pet detective...He killed Big Dan and the fish."

Einhorn clicked off.

"Liar, liar," Ace taunted. "Pants on fire!"

Einhorn smiled cruelly. Then she cocked her police special and pointed it at Ace Ventura's head.

Back at the stadium, Emilio was standing next to Melissa. His police radio crackled to life. Emilio and Melissa listened to the dispatcher's broadcast.

"Attention all units...Code eleven in progress at three hundred forty-three Victorville Road...Officer needs backup...Ace Ventura is wanted for a homicide...Repeat...the suspect's name is Ace Ventura...He is considered armed and dangerous..."

"Oh, my," Melissa cried. She turned to Emilio. "Do you think Ace is in danger?"

Emilio looked grim. "Don't worry," he told Melissa. "I've known Ace for a long time. He's one of the bravest men I know. Ace can handle anything."

"Pleeheeheeheeheeeezzzz don't kill me!" Ace begged. "Nooooo...*Don't kill me!*"

The pet detective was on his knees, both arms wrapped around Lieutenant Einhorn's legs. His cheeks were wet with tears.

"I'll never tell..." Ace pleaded. Then he pointed at Big Dan. "Kill him! He's the one you want!"

"No way," Big Dan protested. "Kill him!"

"Oh, *sure!*" Ace spat. "I come in here to rescue you, and you tell her to *kill* me! *That's* gratitude!"

"Shut up, you stupid *pet detective!*" Big Dan shouted back.

Suddenly a loud gunshot rang out. Both men fell silent and turned to look at Lieutenant Einhorn. She was pointing her gun in the air. There was a new hole in the roof.

"Both of you...*shut up!*" Einhorn shrieked.

Then she smiled again. "We've got a few minutes before my policemen get here. Just enough time for you to watch me kill the fish."

She looked down at Ace, who was still groveling on the floor. "I wouldn't want you to miss *that*, pet boy!"

Meanwhile, Emilio and Melissa were racing down the road in a police car at full speed. The siren was screaming, and other cars were quickly getting out of their way. They were heading for the old ironworks dock on Victorville Road. So was half the Miami police force.

"Hurry, Emilio," Melissa urged. "Are you sure Ace will be okay?" she asked.

"I've known Ace a long time," Emilio answered, "and I've never seen him choke!"

Curious, Melissa asked Emilio how he met the pet detective. Emilio smiled.

"I was just a uniformed cop then," Emilio remembered. "An old blind man on my beat had his Seeing Eye dog stolen by a black market dog ring. The bad guys were selling people's pets for medical experiments. Ace Ventura soon put a stop to that!"

"What happened?" Melissa urged.

"It's a long story," Emilio replied. "But the short version ends with the blind man getting his dog back. That dog was his only friend for fifteen years. I never saw a blind man cry tears of joy before that day. Ace didn't even charge the guy!"

Melissa grew quiet. Then she smiled. Ace had told her that story himself, but she hadn't believed him. Melissa was happy to hear that the story was true. She knew now that Ace was a good man. A *strange* man...but a good one.

Just then Emilio turned a corner sharply. Melissa looked up. She saw the sign for Victorville Road as they flashed by it.

"Pretty cruel," Ace said to Einhorn, "killing a harmless dolphin in cold blood. Afraid you'll buckle under the pressure? *Again?*"

"What would you know about pressure?"

Einhorn asked. She pointed the gun at Ace. As she did, Snowflake popped his head out of the water.

"Oh," Ace mused, "I've done my taxes…"

Einhorn raised the gun to Ace's head. "I've had about all I can take from you," she said. "*Die*, Ventura!"

As Einhorn squeezed the trigger, Snowflake leaped out of the water. The dolphin's tail lashed out and slapped the gun right out of Einhorn's hand. The gun slid across the floor and came to rest in a corner.

Ace saw his chance. Fast as a darting panther, Ace lunged at Einhorn. They locked arms and grappled in the middle of the room.

Ace Ventura was tough, but so was Einhorn! As the police lieutenant broke free, she dodged a punch thrown by the pet detective. Then she held Ace Ventura in a mean headlock.

As Ace struggled helplessly, Einhorn ran his head into the pole that Big Dan was tied to.

Bang! Bang! Bang! Ace's head bounced off

the metal pole again and again.

"Take that," Einhorn howled. "And that, and *that!*"

"Having a little trouble with the lady?" Big Dan asked Ace.

"Listen…oooooffff…tough guy," Ace snarled. "You…oooofffff…don't understand… She's…not a…*aaaaahhhhhh!*"

Einhorn flipped Ace over her head and slammed him to the ground. *Bam!*

But Ace jumped up instantly. The pet detective lashed out with a mean right hook. This one made it to the target—Einhorn got it in the jaw. The lieutenant spun around and crashed to the floor.

Ace dived for the gun, but Einhorn grabbed his leg. Ace tumbled to the floor.

Now Einhorn dived for the gun. Her hand wrapped around the handle, and she picked it up. She turned to point it at the pet detective, but he was gone!

Einhorn looked at Big Dan. He shrugged his shoulders. Einhorn stumbled around the room, searching for her enemy. As she neared the fish tank, there was a huge splash.

Ace Ventura leaped out of the water like a great white shark. His teeth locked on Einhorn's wrist, forcing her to drop the gun into the water. Ace and Einhorn tumbled into a wet heap on the ground.

Suddenly, the doors were knocked down as a horde of cops ran into the room. The police were led by Sergeant Aguado. Emilio and Melissa brought up the rear.

Lieutenant Einhorn jumped to her feet.

"Shoot him!" she cried, pointing to Ace Ventura. The pet detective was just getting to his feet.

But Ace's pal Emilio jumped between the cops and the pet detective.

"Hold your fire!" Emilio shouted. "Don't shoot!"

"Get out of the way, Emilio," Einhorn ordered the policeman. "Ace Ventura kidnapped Snowflake. He killed Roger Podacter, and he was about to kill Big Dan and me!"

But Ace had regained his wits. He turned to the policemen pointing guns at him.

"Ho, ho, ho!" Ace chuckled. "Fiction can be fun! But I find *non*fiction to be much more interesting!

"If you were to look up professional football's all-time bonehead plays," Ace told the cops, "you *might* read about Miami Dolphin player number four...a kicker by the name of Ray Finkle!"

Some of the cops nodded their heads. They remembered that sad day in 1984 when the Miami Dolphins lost the Super Bowl because of a missed field goal.

Ace took a deep breath and continued. "What you might *not* read about is how Ray Finkle lost his mind and was committed to a mental institution, only to escape and join the police force under the assumed identity of a missing hiker, in a diabolical plan to get even with quarterback Big Dan, whom he blamed for the entire thing!"

Ace stopped and gasped for breath. The police looked confused.

"What are you talking about, Ventura?" Sergeant Aguado asked derisively.

"I'm saying that this is *not* Lois Einhorn! She is Ray Finkle...She is a *man!*"

"He's lying!" Einhorn interrupted. "I order you to shoot him!"

"Yeah?" Ace said. "Let's just see who's lying..." Ace reached out and grabbed a handful of Einhorn's long hair.

"Would a real woman need to wear a *wig?*" Ace yanked hard on Einhorn's hair. To the surprise of everyone in the room, Einhorn's hair came off! Under the wig was an athletic buzz cut.

Big Dan gasped in shock. The cops lowered their weapons. There, before them, stood Ray Finkle!

"Roger Podacter was Finkle's old coach," Ace said. "He realized that Lieutenant Einhorn was actually Ray Finkle when 'she' showed up to investigate Snowflake's kidnapping...and he was murdered for it. Lois Einhorn *is* Ray Finkle. And I have the proof!"

Ace grabbed Finkle's hand and pulled off the Super Bowl ring he was wearing. He held up the ring so everyone could see that it was

117

missing one of the gemstones—the stone that Ace had found in Snowflake's tank the day after the kidnapping.

Ray Finkle began to holler insanely. "It's all Big Dan's fault!" he screamed. "The laces were in! *The laces were in!*"

Several policemen took Ray Finkle by the arms. They handcuffed him and led him out to a waiting squad car.

Sergeant Aguado walked up to the pet detective. He shook Ace's hand.

"I don't know how you did it, Ventura," the sergeant said. "But that was mighty good police work. If you ever need a job on the *real* police force, give me a call."

"Thanks, Sergeant," Ace replied graciously. "But I don't do humans."

Melissa ran up to Ace and threw her arms around him. "You did it, Ace!" she cried. "You did it!"

"Not quite yet," the pet detective answered. "We still have to get Snowflake... and this other guy...down to the stadium!"

*   *   *

A dozen police cars—and a large truck with a pool of water in the back—rushed down the highway. They were heading for the stadium. The Super Bowl was starting in only a few minutes.

At the head of the pack, Ace Ventura drove his rusty Chevy Bel Air. Melissa was in the front seat next to Ace. Big Dan, the quarterback, was in the back.

Big Dan shook his head in admiration. "Hey, Ace!" the Miami Dolphins quarterback said.

"Yeah, Dan?" Ace replied.

"You're a weird guy, Ventura!" Dan said. "A great pet detective, but a truly weird guy!"

"Why, thank you, Dan!" Ace Ventura said with pride.

13

A Great Humanitarian and a Lover of All Animals

Super Bowl Sunday was in full swing at Dolphin Stadium. The sun shone brightly. The Goodyear blimp floated overhead. The cheerleaders cheered, and the football players rushed out onto the field to the cries of their fans.

All was right in America.

And all was right for the Miami team too.

Only minutes before, the announcer had broadcast the news over the loudspeakers. Television delivered the word to millions of viewers. Snowflake the dolphin and Big Dan the quarterback were saved!

Down on the field the teams were lined up for the coin toss. Ace Ventura and Melissa were at the fifty-yard line, smiling and laughing. They were enjoying the awesome spectacle, just like all the other fans across the nation.

Everyone's attention was fixed on the giant television board. There flashed the words WELCOME BACK, SNOWFLAKE AND BIG DAN! The crowd roared loudly. Only Emilio missed the bulletin. He was talking to a pretty cheerleader.

As the fans cheered, Ace looked at Melissa. She returned his gaze. Then, for the first time, they kissed.

But suddenly Ace caught sight of something that set his pet detective radar humming. He couldn't believe what he saw!

There, perched on a big tub of Gatorade, was the rare white pigeon.

"Duty calls," Ace whispered to Melissa. She looked at Ace, puzzled. But the pet detective was already in action. He crept slowly across the field, carefully inching toward the pigeon.

Just as Ace was about to grab the rare bird, a man in a green eagle suit walked up for a drink. He waved his arm at the pigeon, scaring the valuable bird into flight.

"*Noooooo!*" Ace wailed. As the pigeon shot into the air, Ace made a hopeless grab for it.

And missed.

Ace was fuming. The pet detective strolled over to the man in the bird suit.

"Thanks a lot, Polly," Ace snapped at the costumed figure. It was the other team's mascot. "You just cost me twenty-five thousand bucks!"

"Tough luck, jerk!" the man in the bird suit replied. "That bird was in my way."

"Reeheeheeheelyyy?" Ace said.

"Beat it!" the man in the bird suit barked. He pushed the pet detective out of the way.

Ace pushed back.

Pretty soon Ace and the man in the green eagle suit were exchanging punches.

Just then, the loudspeakers blasted out another announcement.

"Ladies and gentlemen," the voice on the loudspeaker said. "The National Football League would now like to offer a very special thank-you to the man who rescued Big Dan and our beloved Snowflake...a great humani-

tarian and a lover of animals everywhere…
Mr. Ace Ventura, pet detective!"

The cameras all turned and focused on
Ace. The big television board showed the picture to the entire stadium. That same picture
was broadcast all over the nation—and all
over the world.

It was the image of Ace Ventura, the now-
renowned pet detective—the lover of animals
everywhere—sitting on top of the man in the
eagle suit, pounding the feathers off him!

Ace Ventura's spine tingled. He felt all the
eyes in the stadium watching him. He
stopped pummeling the bird man. Ace looked
up sheepishly. Then he smiled his goofy smile
and waved to the cameras.

"All rightee then!" Ace shouted to his
adoring fans.

It was a fitting end to another adventure in
the life of the world's greatest—and *only*—pet
detective!

Be sure to check out Ace's next exciting case:

"Since the disappearance of Shikaka, the sacred bat," Greenwall explained, "the Wachatis think the god of the caves is angry with them."

Ace paled. "Bat?" he asked nervously. "What bat?"

Greenwall looked puzzled. "Why, the bat you're here to find."

"Hey, buddy!" Ace said. "I'm here to find a Shikaka. You didn't say anything about a *bat!*"

"The Shikaka *is* a bat. What difference does it make?" Greenwall asked.

"What difference does it make!" Ace cried, amazed. "Have you ever seen a bat? They're disgusting!"

"Does this mean you won't take the case?"

"Oh, I'll find it," Ace answered. "I just won't *touch* it!"